Christmas FARM

MARY LYN RAY ★ Illustrated by BARRY ROOT

HARCOURT, INC.

Orlando Austin New York San Diego London

Requests for permission to make copies of any part of the work should be
submitted online at www.harcourt.com/contact or mailed to the following address:
Permissions Department, Houghton Mifflin Harcourt Publishing Company,
6277 Sea Harbor Drive, Orlando, Florida 32887-6777.

www.HarcourtBooks.com

Library of Congress Cataloging-in-Publication Data
Ray, Mary Lyn.
Christmas farm/Mary Lyn Ray; illustrated by Barry Root.
p.   cm.
Summary: Wilma decides to plant Christmas trees with the help of her young neighbor, Parker.
[1. Christmas trees—Fiction.   2. Gardening—Fiction.]   I. Root, Barry, ill.   II. Title.
PZ7.R210154Ch   2008
[E]—dc22   2007015216
ISBN 978-0-15-216290-0

First edition
A C E G H F D B

Printed in Singapore

The illustrations in this book were done in watercolor and gouache on Arches 140 lb. Hot Press Paper.
The display type was set in Canterbury Old Style.
The text type was set in Minister Std. Book.
Color separations by SC Graphic Technology Pte Ltd, Singapore
Printed and bound by Tien Wah Press, Singapore
Production supervision by Pascha Gerlinger
Designed by Linda Lockowitz

For my sister,
who first showed me the mysteries
among the green branches

—M. L. R.

★

In memory of Sarah Westbrook

—B. R.

Wilma had grown petunias and sunflowers for years.
She was ready to graduate to something else.

But she couldn't decide what.

When snow fell on the last sunflower stalks, Wilma still didn't know how to make her garden different next year. And now there was Christmas to think of.

On her back hill, Wilma had looked in July for the right tree to cut in December. Her Christmas began when she went for the one she had chosen and brought it home to her parlor.

But before she wrapped the green branches with lights, she thought of people who had no back hill. Where would *they* find such a fine tree?

Then Wilma knew. She knew what to plant instead of petunias. She needed a shovel, string, scissors, time. She needed good brown earth.

She had them all.

So Wilma ordered sixty-two dozen small starts of balsam for spring. She was pretty good at counting by dozens. When she made doughnuts on Saturday mornings, she always made a dozen. But *sixty-two* dozen was a lot of trees.

She would need help setting them out.

She would need Parker.

Parker lived next door. He was five, like the seedlings.
Every Fourth of July, Wilma and Parker made a parade,
waving flags and banging on pots and pans. At Halloween
they made jack-o'-lanterns.

Parker had helped Wilma grow sunflowers.

He would help again.

As soon as the ground was warm, Wilma and Parker began.
Using balls of string, they measured twenty-four straight rows.

Then they dug sixty-two dozen holes.
And they planted sixty-two dozen trees:
seven hundred and forty-four trees.

"Will they be ready by Christmas?" asked Parker.

"*Nooooo,*" said Wilma. The trees had to grow—through the summer, the fall, the winter, the spring. And then they had to grow some more.

While they grew, Parker told the trees about Christmas. He knew all about Christmas.

To keep the grass from covering their trees, he and
Wilma weeded around each one.

Then October's leaves blew across the trees, and
November's snow began to fall.

Before winter's end, some of the trees were lost
to mice that ate their stems and roots.

But seven hundred and
nineteen remained.

The young trees woke with the spring, and again Wilma and Parker weeded around them, and Parker told them things. Now that he was six, he knew even more than when he was five.

On summer nights, brown moths fluttered among the trees, fireflies flickered above them, and whip-poor-wills called across the darkness.

Then fall came again. And winter.

During the long, cold months, some of the trees were lost to deer that dug in the snow to chew the sweet green tips. But six hundred and seventy-three survived.

When Parker came to help with spring chores, Wilma had been shopping. For a tractor.

She chose a blue one with a horn, though there was nothing to honk at except the sky, the ring of mountains, yellow dandelions—and Parker. Wilma let him try the horn. Parker would have liked to drive the tractor, too, but seven wasn't old enough for that.

The trees weren't old enough, either.

When Christmas came, they were still too small to cut.

So they slept through another winter.

Again some were lost to mice and deer, storm and ice.
But when spring came, there were six hundred and fifty-two
left. Wilma mowed. Parker ran among the rows, counting. Six
hundred and fifty-two was a big number to count, but Parker
could do it now that he was eight.

All summer, bobolinks decorated the trees with song.

Then fall came, winter came, snow came.

Moose cracked some of the branches and chewed them.

But six hundred and seventeen trees survived.

That summer the trees were nine. It was time to shape them. Wilma and Parker worked together. Now that he was nine, Parker could reach almost as high as Wilma.

Some of the trees they left as their branches had grown, for people who liked trees that way. The rest they trimmed round and round, for people who liked them *that* way. Soon the trees would be Christmas trees.

One more winter the trees slept under snow. Only two were lost to ice, eleven to moose, and seven to deer. But five hundred and ninety-seven remained.

It was a busy spring for a boy and for trees turning ten. Parker and Wilma painted a sign. It said Christmas Farm. Then they built a stand. And they bought tags—fifty dozen.

At the end of summer, they put up a second sign.

It said Trees For Sale.

Some people came in August to choose a tree and tag it.

Some came in October. More came in November.

The most came in December.

All month, Wilma and Parker were cutting and carrying and sledding trees and making change from the money box. They sold three hundred and fifty-six trees.

Then a family who had a Christmas tree lot in the city
came and bought another two hundred and ten, filling their
big red truck to the top.

At last it was time for Parker and Wilma to choose
their trees.

That night, across their yards, Christmas twinkled.

Far away, too, in rooms they never saw, in places they never knew, five hundred and sixty-six trees that Wilma and Parker had grown wore lights and balls and tinsel in their branches—green balsam branches that smelled the sweet smell of Christmas.

Back on the hill, the twenty-nine trees that weren't chosen began winter again.

Parker told them they would grow tallest, for people who wanted tall trees next year.

By spring, new green would appear where each cut tree had been. One tiny sprout would become a new trunk. The trees would grow back on their own.

But some sprouts might be crooked. Some might be chewed. And there was room on the farm to start more.

So one Saturday night, each eating a doughnut, Wilma and Parker filled out an order for eighty-three dozen new seedlings.

Then they waited for spring.

A NOTE FROM THE AUTHOR

When I was growing up in the South, I dreamed of living in the land of Christmas trees. Now, on an old farm in New Hampshire, I do. Like Wilma, all summer, when I go into the woods, I'm looking for the right tree to cut in December.

The idea of an ever-green tree dressed with light and color is much older than Christmas. The oldest myths tell of trees blooming with flowers in winter's dark, and illumined with the light that returns at the solstice. These trees were a symbol of life reborn. So when Christmas began to be celebrated, the decorated tree was incorporated into Christmas teachings and custom.

Long familiar in Europe, Christmas trees were rarely seen in the United States until 1820 or 1830; but by 1850 they were becoming more common. In 1856, President Franklin Pierce had the first Christmas tree in the White House. By 1880, some two hundred thousand trees (which farmers cut from roadsides and forests) were being sold in New York City, and that number multiplied around the country. Worried about the protection of forests, President Theodore Roosevelt declared there would be no White House tree in 1901. When his children objected, he eventually gave in,

but he addressed the long-term issues by urging the growing of Christmas trees on intentional tree farms. Many people had the same concern. That same year, whether for market advantage, convenience in harvesting, or good conservation practice, a commercial Christmas tree farm was operating in New Jersey—with customers coming to tag their trees, which were later delivered to them—and quickly the concept spread.

Most Christmas trees are now grown as a farm crop, like potatoes or pumpkins. Each year some thirty million—including balsams, Fraser firs, Douglas firs, spruces, Scotch pines, and other species—are harvested on twenty-one thousand commercial tree farms and smaller family tree lots in the United States. Trees planted as seedlings ensure a renewable supply and, in many instances, allow farmers to make use of land that can't carry other crops. But tree farms don't provide just Christmas trees. They are rich habitat for animals and birds and wildflowers. And their green rows—waiting, growing—remind us, too, that the year will come again to December and all the ancient mystery December brings us to.

—M. L. R.

CHRISTMAS TREE GROWTH RATE

81 inches
66 inches
54 inches
39 inches
27 inches
12 inches

5 years 6 years 7 years 8 years 9 years 10 years